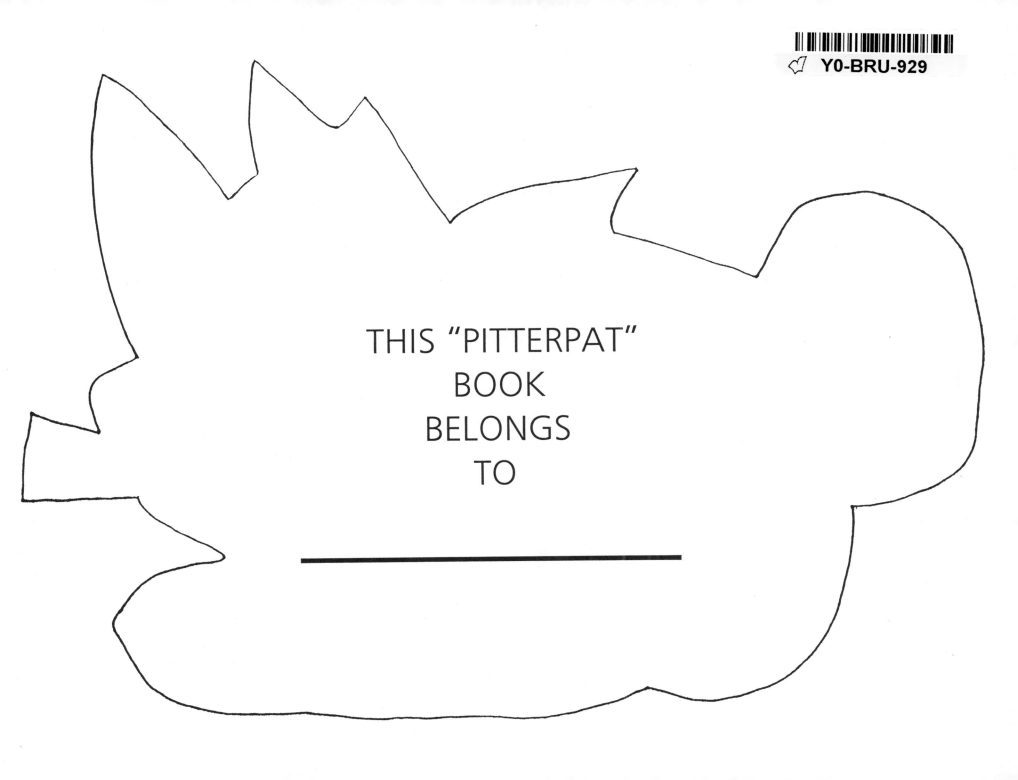

THIS "PITTERPAT"
BOOK
BELONGS
TO

_____

PITTERPAT

**Written and illustrated
by Lee Carolynn Jacobson**

A Book For Those Who Have Been Sexually Abused and Those Who Love Them

For information write:

Hampton Roads Publishing Co., Inc.
891 Norfolk Square
Norfolk, VA 23502

Or call: (804)459-2453
FAX: (804)455-8907

ISBN 1-878901-85-0

Printed on acid-free paper in the United States of America

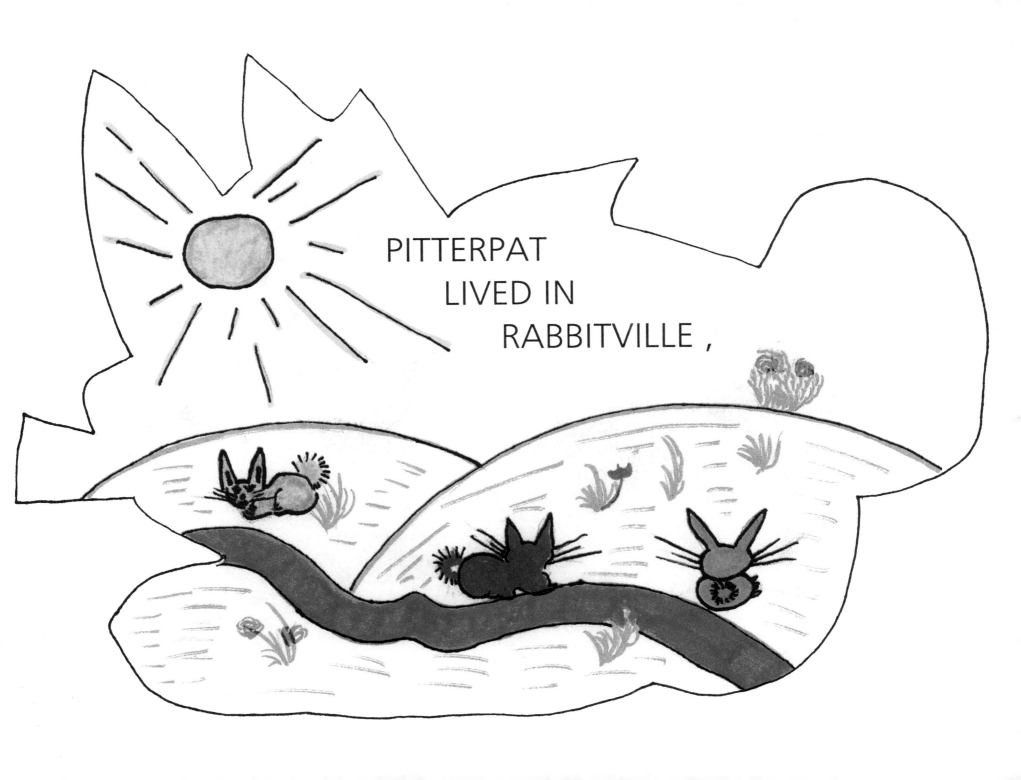

PITTERPAT
LIVED IN
RABBITVILLE ,

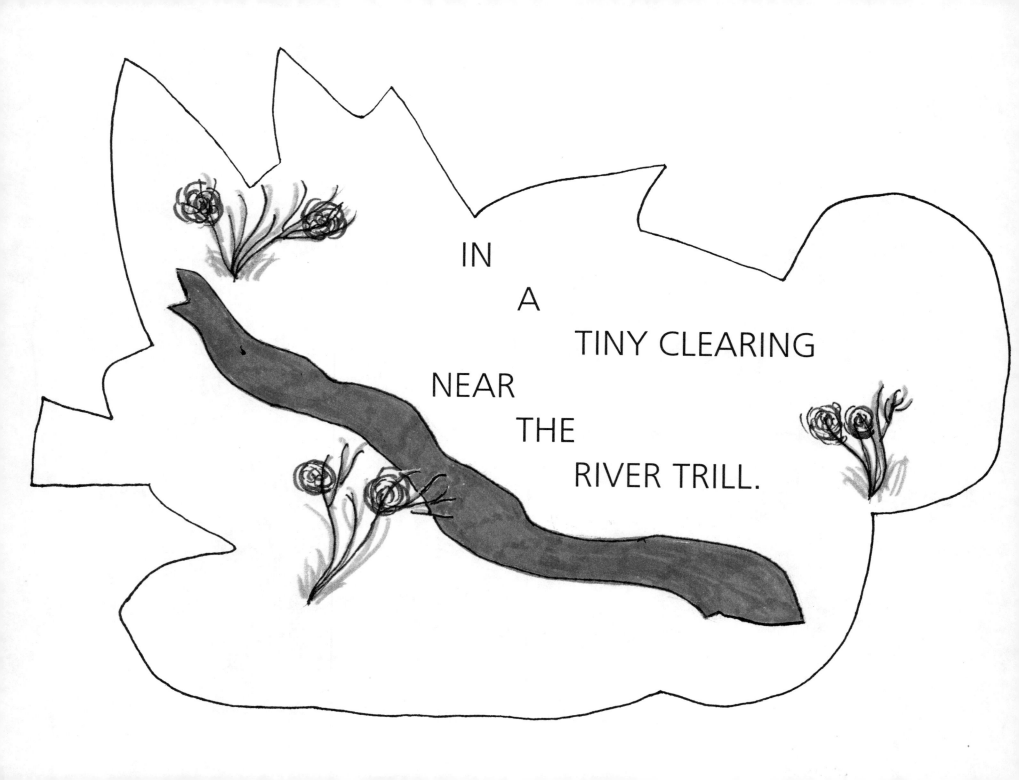

IN

A

TINY CLEARING

NEAR

THE

RIVER TRILL.

AND EVERY DAY

HER FRIENDS WOULD

STOP BY

HER HOME

AND SAY,

AND

THEY

WOULD

HOP AND PLAY

WITH BUTTERFLIES

AND BIRDS

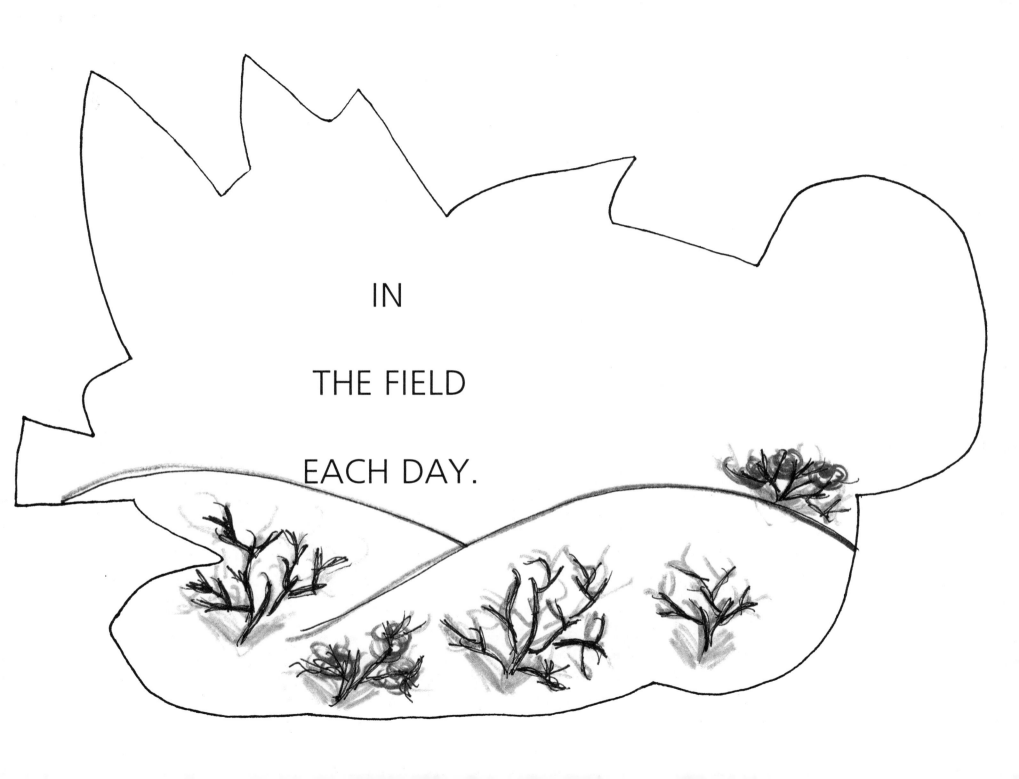

IN

THE FIELD

EACH DAY.

ONE DAY

PITTERPAT COULDN'T

COME OUT AND PLAY.

SHE WAS EXCITED.

"RELATIVES
ARE COMING,"

ONE BUNNY

WAS <u>BIG</u>

AND LOOKED KIND OF

MEAN!!

HE

STOLE INTO

PITTERPAT'S ROOM

AT NIGHT

WITHOUT BEING

SEEN!!

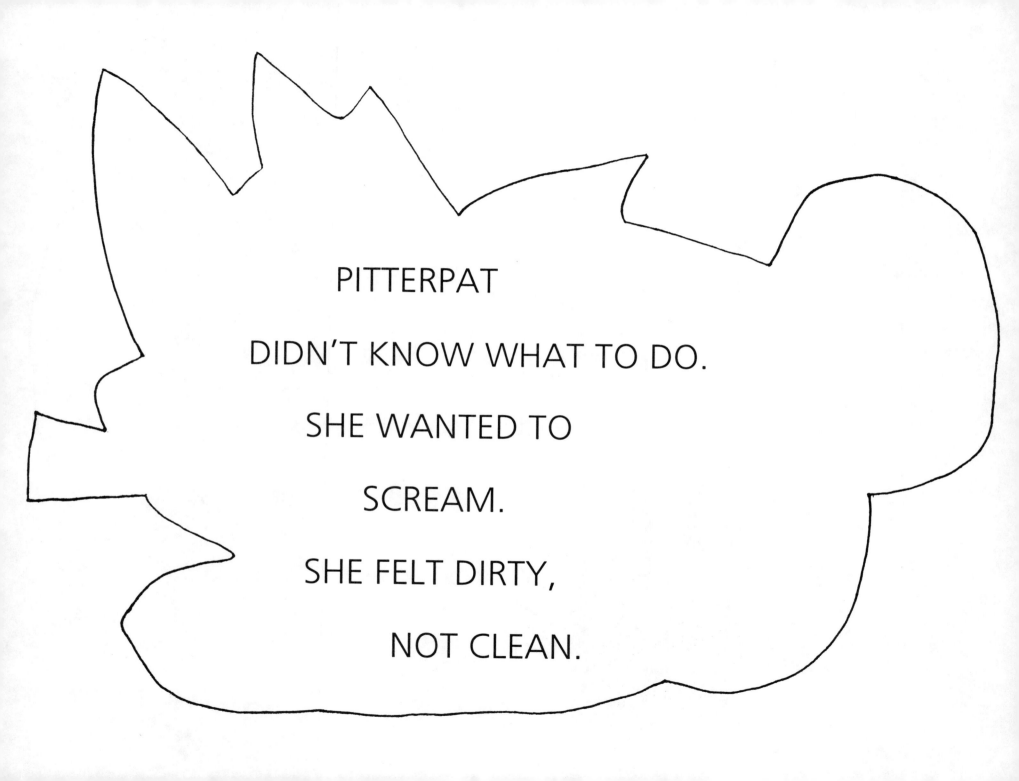

PITTERPAT

DIDN'T KNOW WHAT TO DO.

SHE WANTED TO

SCREAM.

SHE FELT DIRTY,

NOT CLEAN.

SHE

CRIED.

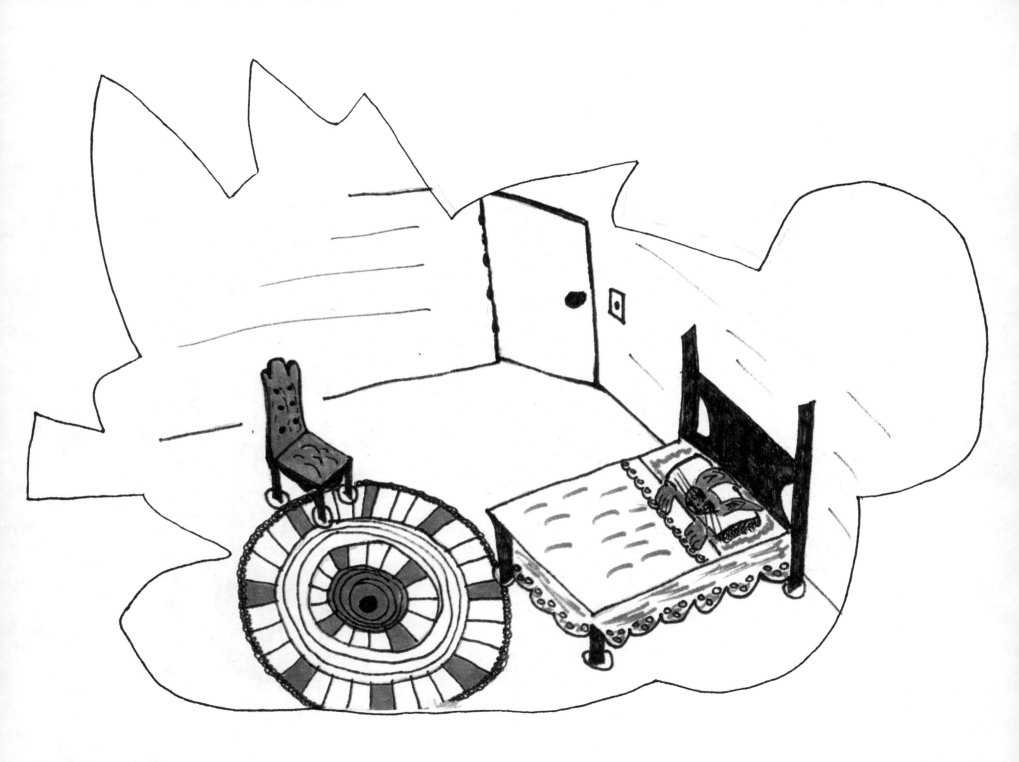

PITTERPAT
GOT QUIET

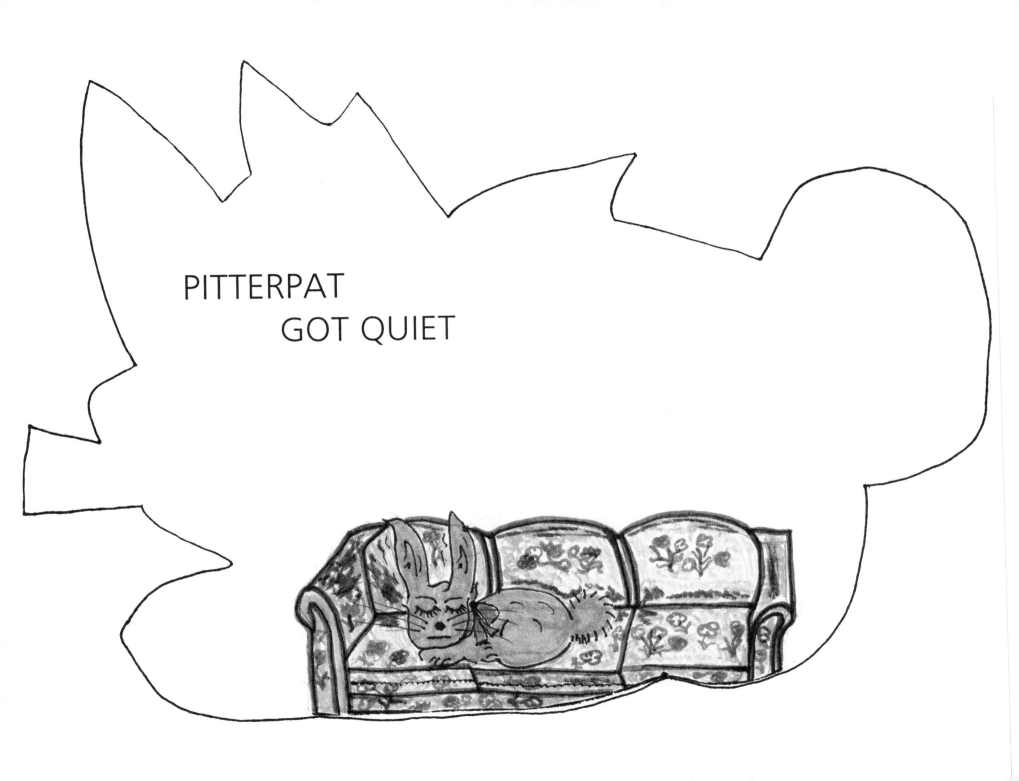

AND

DIDN'T WANT

TO PLAY.

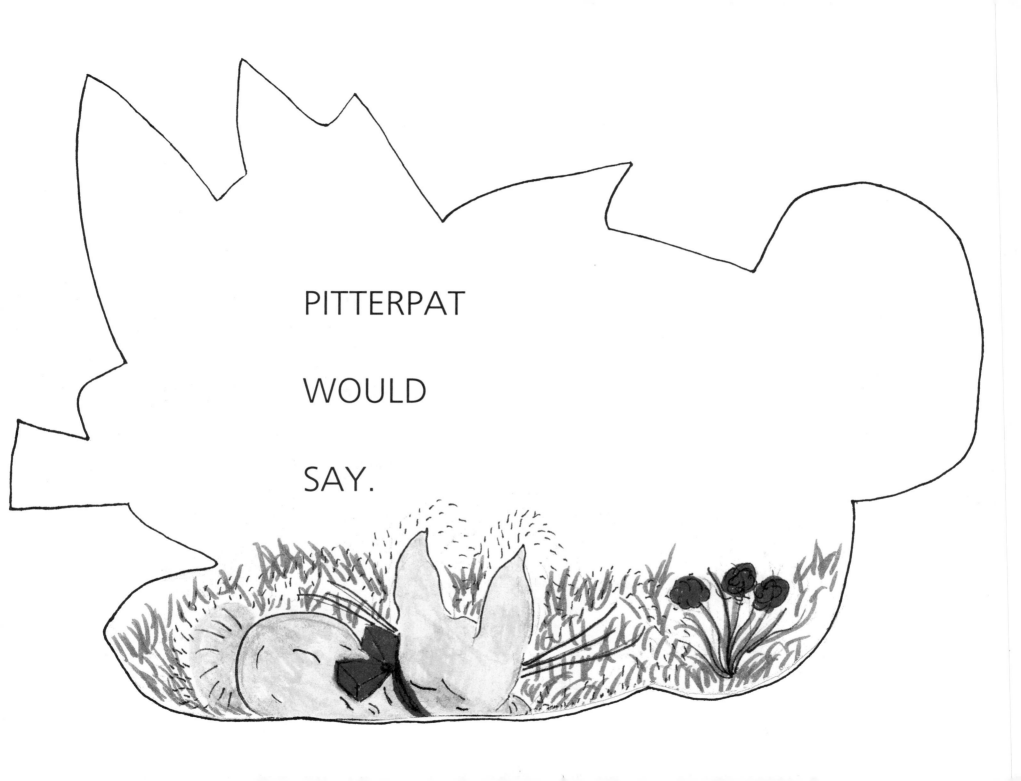

PITTERPAT

WOULD

SAY.

THE

RELATIVES

LEFT

AND THE

DAYS

WENT

BY.

PITTERPAT

WAS NUMB.

SHE DIDN'T

LAUGH

OR

CRY.

THE

MEAN RABBIT

HAD TOLD

HER NOT TO

TELL.

SHE STAYED

BY HERSELF.

SHE DIDN'T FEEL

WELL.

THEN

ONE

DAY,

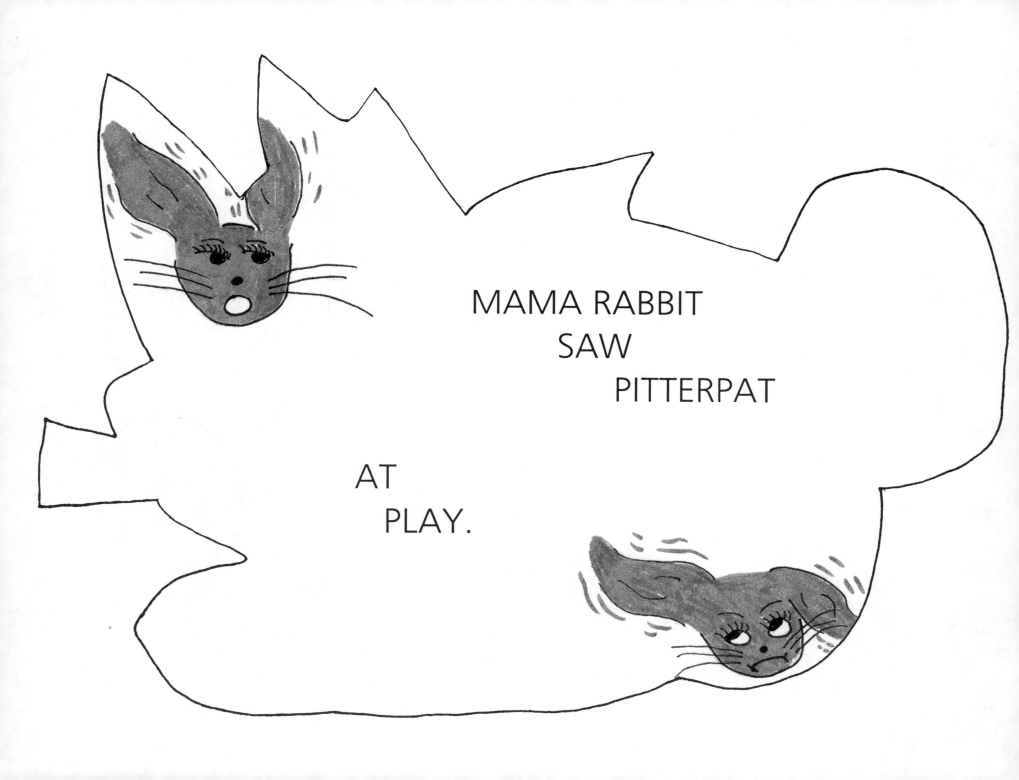

MAMA RABBIT
SAW
PITTERPAT

AT
PLAY.

SHE SAW HER

TOUCH HER DOLLS

IN THE SAME

WAY.

PITTERPAT

NODDED.

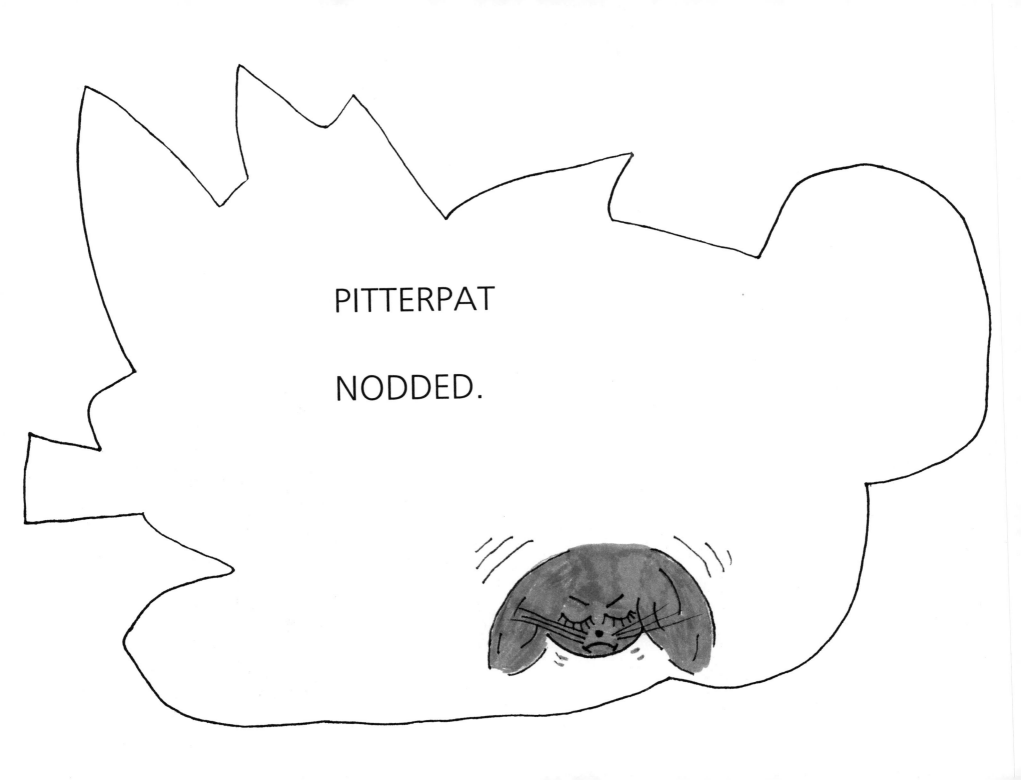

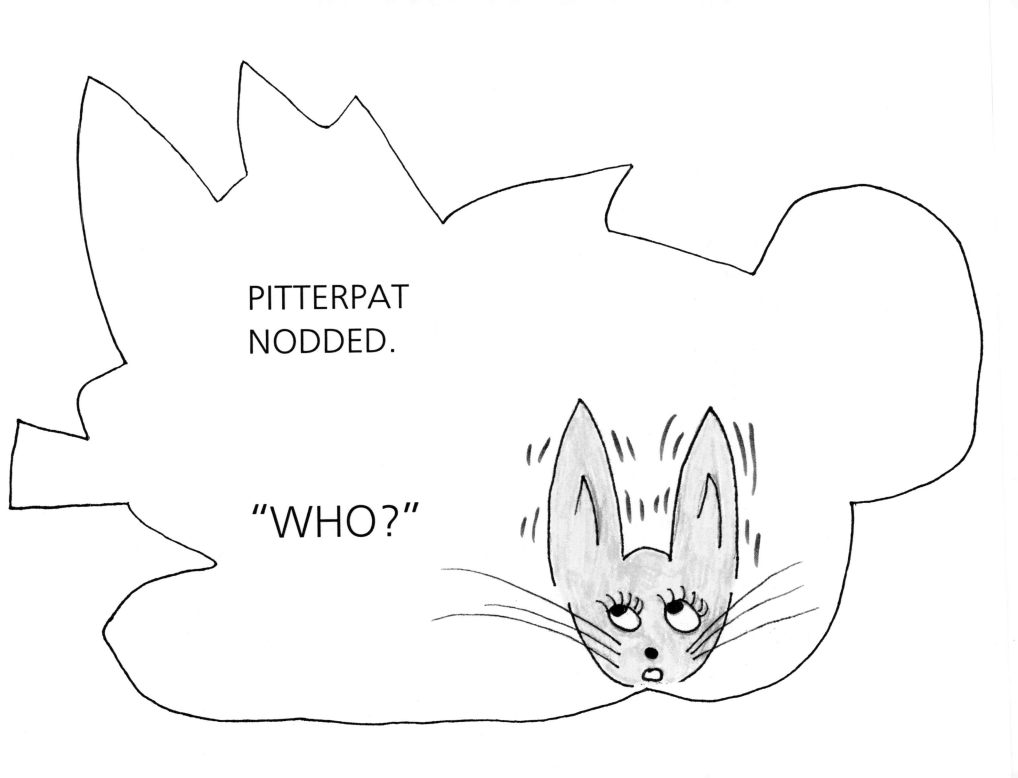

AND —
PITTERPAT
TOLD HER

EVERYTHING,

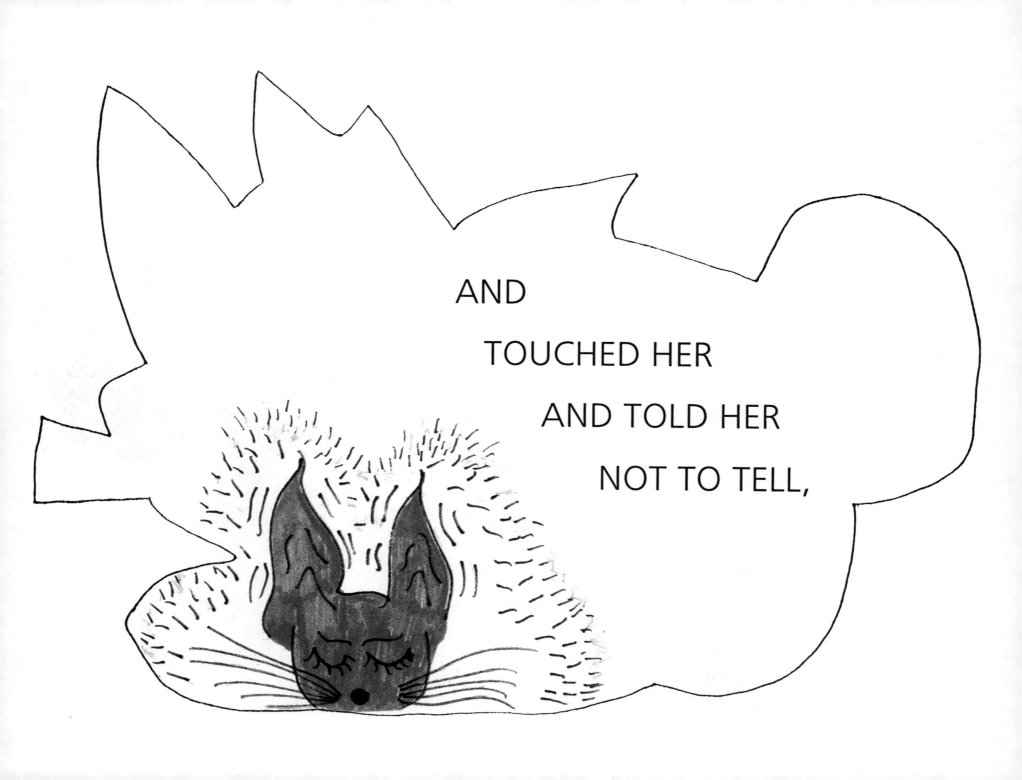

AND

TOUCHED HER

AND TOLD HER

NOT TO TELL,

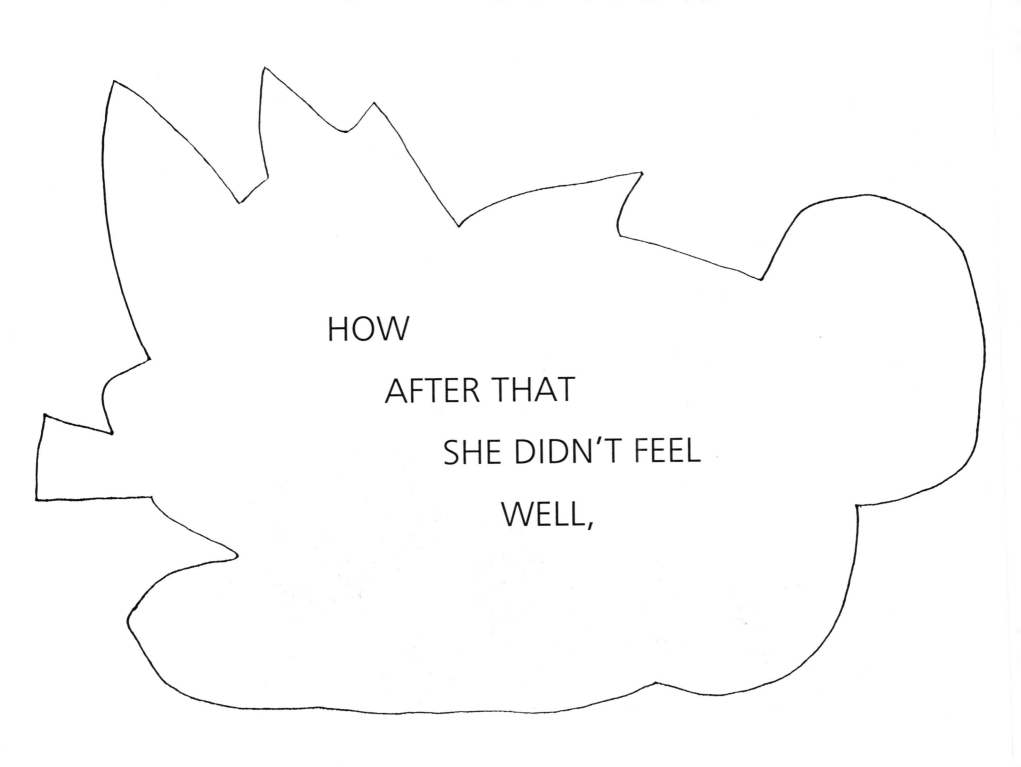

HOW

AFTER THAT

SHE DIDN'T FEEL

WELL,

HOW SHE WAS

SAD

AND FELT SO BAD.

AND

MAMA RABBIT

HUGGED HER AND

CRIED

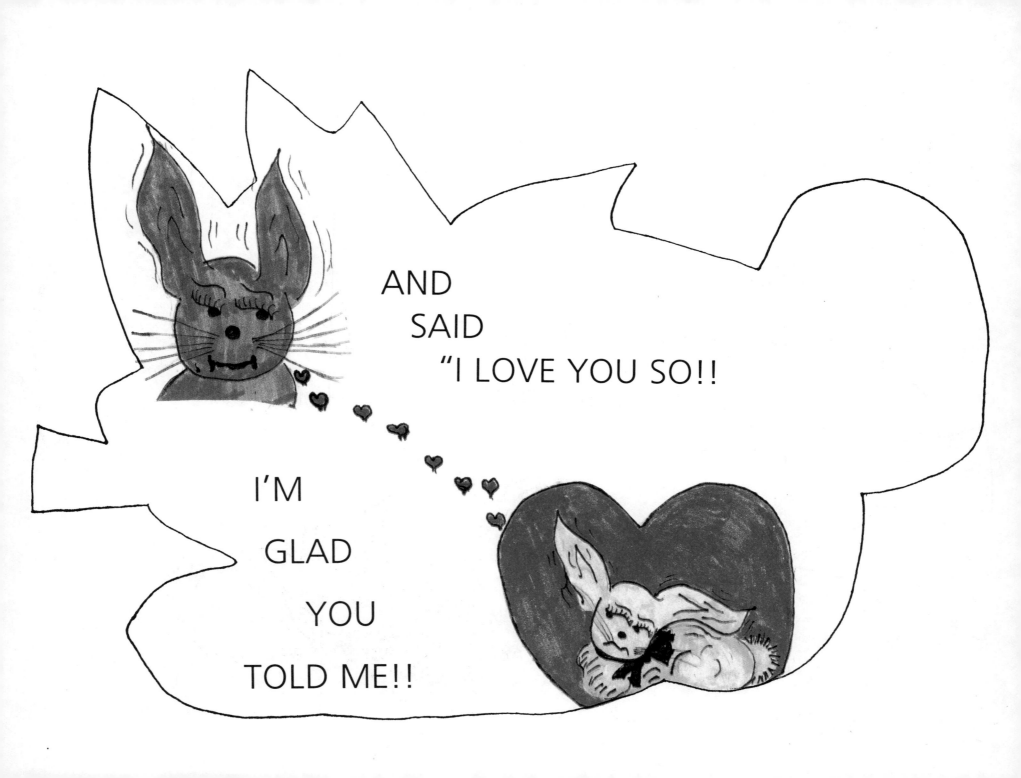

AND

WHAT MAMA RABBIT

SAID

WAS

TRUE!!

HE

WOULD

PAY!!

"PITTERPAT!! PITTERPAT!! COME OUT AND PLAY!!," HER FRIENDS WOULD SAY.

AND

PITTERPAT WOULD SAY,

"OKAY!!

OKAY!!"

Author's Note

Recovery from sexual abuse includes asking the right questions. I have written an 8-page pamphlet with questions which are designed to aid the victims of sexual abuse and their families and friends. The story of Pitterpat promotes the open discussion of sexual abuse and its effects. The questions provide an opportunity for the identification of possible victims. The answers to these questions can alert an adult to the presence of abuse, and help a child to begin the recovery process. Gestures and comments, eyes and actions, all provide clues to what may be occurring in your own families. In the non-threatening forum of the third-person context, it is possible for victims to attribute to Pitterpat personal situations and emotions they aren't yet able to openly discuss with others. Trauma can be transferred to Pitterpat and options of recovery discussed with detachment.

Nearly everyone has been affected by abusive situations. The education of family and friends is an aid to recovery. The questions in this pamphlet invite the participation of all, not just the victims and their therapists or families. Empathy for the victim is elicited by discussion and education, and a better understanding of traumatic response is possible. A change in behavior doesn't indicate a change in affection. To avoid compounding the victims' initial betrayal with rejection and accusation, it is necessary to educate family and friends to what traumatic response is and how to react to the behavior changes. These questions are designed to provide a non-threatening forum where communication can occur. *Pitterpat* is focused on recovery. Asking the right questions can help initiate tentative steps of recovery. Remember: recovery is a process, and it *can* be accomplished. If you're interested in the pamphlet, please write the publisher for details, or call (804) 459-2453.